His Fae's Protector

Reverse Harem Academy Romance

Amelia Wilson

Contents

Prologue

The elevator hissed and hummed as it climbed higher. Each new floor caused the small box to rattle, startling the occupants inside. But it wasn't like the three women heading to the top floor could be killed by such a device. No, they were more than fragile mortal souls. They were the furies of hell itself, summoned to the top of the empire.

"I'm surprised he summoned you here, Arae. Weren't you supposed to be busy tormenting the humans?" The slender and graceful of the three snickered as she glanced at her fingernails and plucked the dirt out from under them.

"You really think I would pass up an opportunity like this?" Arae answered throwing her braided hair back over her shoulder. Although she wasn't nearly as lean as her older sister, she still had looks to kill. In fact, any of the three women in the elevator would be more than thrilled to take out a human the old fashion way. Death by insanity was their specialty after all and they'd kill to be able to unleash the old ways.

"Apparently neither of you actually read the invitation," the youngest of the three said shaking her head. She crossed her arms over her chest and glared at her older sister Arae first, then Delphine.

"Leave it to Set to get all technical," Delphine teased as she slapped Arae's hand in a high five. Set stood in the corner of the elevator counting the numbers as the elevator continued to rattle higher up the shaft.

"Oh, I think you made her mad," Arae snickered as Set's eyes lingered on the numbers as her blood began to boil. Under her skin she tried desperately to remain calm, but it never worked out that way. Not when her sisters were there to egg her on.

"Delphine," Set's lips barely moved as she kept her eyes locked on the number. "Will you please keep your snide comments to yourself?"

"Or what?" Delphine glared at Set as her hand rose. A flicker and spark billowed up in the palm of Delphine's hand as she formed a tiny fireball. Set side-glanced to find the ball no bigger than an apple bobbing in her sister's hand. Shaking her head Set nodded and pressed her lips into a tight line.

The ball of flames bouncing about crackled and hissed as the fire extinguished and turned into a ball of ice.

Arae clapped her hands watching her sisters duel. Delphine dropped her hand quickly and the ice ball plummeted to the floor of the elevator and shattered into a million pieces.

"You think you have what it takes to take me on?" Delphine said throwing her shoulders back.

"Sisters, come on now," Arae pleaded as she stepped between Delphine and Set. "Why don't we save ourselves for the actual battle, huh?"

"You are so stupid, Arae," Delphine hissed stepping back and turning her venom on Arae. "When was the last time any of us have seen battle? When was the last the gods even called us to assist them? It's been nearly a millennium."

"Well," Arae stepped into the small corner of the elevator and nodded as her eyes darted to her sisters. "Maybe there is something going on we don't know about. Something that only requires our unique skill sets," Arae shrugged trying to keep herself in neutral territory as Set glared daggers at Delphine.

"Arae is right," Set said with a crooked little smile playing at the corner of her lips. "We have been called because of our skill set. The only question is, what exactly does he want us to do?"

"I thought you had all the answers," Delphine grumbled turning her back on Set as she spoke. Arae flashed a hopeful smile to Set as the elevator rocked as it stopped. The sisters breathed in a collective sigh as the doors opened.

"Well, one way or another, we are about to find out what he wants," Arae said stepping out of the elevator first. The large marble floors soothed her hot feet as she stepped closer to the living room. It had been forever since the three of them had set eyes on such a place. Everything was exquisite and polished, even the brass statues that lingered in the corners to the paintings hanging on the walls. The sisters gasped to see such a sight as they made their way deeper into the penthouse suite.

"Ah ladies, you all came. Wonderful." The gentle coaxing sound of his voice sent chills through the sisters. They turned on their heels and bowed low as the tan man in a dark kimono sashayed down the hallway.

"Delphine it's so nice to see you again," he said curling his strong arm around the slender sister and pulling him closer to him. She cooed as the heat of his body warmed hers. She shivered as her lips quivered to brush against his. He smiled as he stole a moment with her. Arae and Set watched as Andrew held their sister in an intimate embrace before letting her go.

Delphine blushed as Andrew released her back into the custody of her sisters. Set and Arae glared at Delphine as questions lingered in their eyes about the exchanged.

"I'm thrilled you all have come tonight," Andrew said winking at Arae. Set glanced to her right only to find Arae stifling her giggles as she looked at him.

"What is it you want?" Set asked holding her shoulders back. Jealousy filled her as she spoke to him. Clearly she was not a part of his inner circle the way her sisters seemed to be.

"I have a job for you?" he answered as he moved past the sisters and walked into the living room. Delphine led behind him as Arae tried to wrestle her way to the front of the pack. Set shook her head and remained behind the three of them waiting for the shoe to drop.

In the pit of her stomach she felt there was something not quiet right about the whole situation. Or perhaps it was her jealousy feeding her mistrust, either way she remained distant as Andrew took a seat on the leather couch and opened his arms for Set's sisters to snuggle into him.

"What exactly is the job?" Set asked moving to the large windows that stretched from floor to ceiling. She stared out into the vast city lights that twinkled like stars.

"That is what I always loved about you Set, you get straight to the point," Andrew said. Set could hear the smile in his voice and noticed he stared at her through the dark reflection of the window.

"I want you three to take care of a little problem for me," he said nuzzling into Arae's neck. The girl giggled as Andrew tickled her on the couch.

"Keep going?" Set said tapping her foot as she crossed her arms. It was clear she was the third wheel and only here to keep things moving forward. For a moment she wondered what would have happened if she hadn't been there. Would her sisters be able to stay focused long enough to hear the plan? Or would they become too distracted by the power Andrew held?

Set shook her head and turned on her heels. Her eyebrow arched as she waited for the snogging to cease. Her eyes widened as the arm around Delphine slipped around her tiny frame of a body. Just as his fingers brushed against Delphine's chest Set cleared her throat.

"The problem?" Set asked holding Andrew's gaze. "I doubt it has anything to do with what is in your pants at the moment."

"Actually, it does have something to do with that," Andrew said coughing and releasing Arae and Delphine. He scooted back on the couch and folded the kimono over his chest to hide his pecks.

"Apparently I have an offspring," Andrew said.

"That's wonderful," Delphine said clapping her hands as she lit up.

"No, it's not. The boy is mortal. He is nothing like me, nothing at all. It is because he is so weak and human," Andrew spit the word human like a curse as his hands balled into tight fists. "I want him gone. I can't have an offspring of mine be so... so... well, human."

Andrew shot up from the couch sending Arae and Delphine flying back from him. Only Set remained standing, her eyes smoldering with boredom.

"A human? You want us to take out a human? Do you know how beneath us that is? We once laid armies to waste and you are using us to take out a boy?"

"Do not underestimate him," Andrew shouted. The beams of the ceiling rumbled under the weight of his voice. Set glanced to her sisters. A wicked smile turned the corners of Delphine's lips up as Arae rubbed her hands together.

"Very well," Set said turning her attention back to Andrew. "It will be done."

"Oh and make sure you use the proper channels. I wouldn't want the news getting out about this. It would look bad on at the polls."

"Of course," Arae cooed as Andrew relaxed once more between Arae and Delphine. Set shook her head as Arae grazed her fingers over Andrew's chest and nuzzled into him.

"What is it in for us?" Set asked lifting her head a bit higher. "Granted the job isn't too strenuous, still we should be compensated for our time."

"Of course, of course," Andrew said waving his hand. Two servants walked into the room carrying an enormous chest. Set watched the two men struggle with it until they dropped it at her feet.

"I'm sure you have wanted this for a while now," Andrew said smirking as he glimpsed Set through the corner of his eye.

Set breathed in deeply as she placed her hands over the top of the chest. Every fiber in her body tingled as she pried opened the chest and peered inside of it. Her mouth dropped as her eyes widened.

"We will do as you ask," Set said beyond astonished by the contents.

"Not so fast, you only get that when the task is complete," Andrew said with a chuckle as he clapped his hands. Before Set could reach inside to snag the golden spear, it was gone.

"Sisters," Set dropped her voice as she glanced to Arae then Delphine. "Are you with me?"

"Of course sister," they said in unison.

"Then we have a human to dispose of," Set said rising.

"And ladies, do use whatever means necessary won't you? I don't care if the boy ends up in an institution for the rest of his life, or if he commits suicide. Just get rid of him."

Delphine and Arae rose and moved to stand beside their sister Set. For a brief moment they each exchanged a silent covenant before turning to face Andrew. A smile played at the corner of his lips as they nodded.

"It will be done."

Chapter 1

An aching numbness clenched my heart as I clung to the wooden pole. My eyes darted about scanning the area as the clatter of laughter broke my concentration. Whipping my head around I glared at Molly and Shannon, my two best friends who, if memory served me right, would often get me into far too much trouble.

Molly batted her long purple lashes as her lush lips curled at the corners mischievously. The rapid beating of her wings cooled the burning in my cheeks as I shook my head and turned my attention to the lovely Shannon. Every guy on campus wanted Shannon. Not because of her long legs that stretched up to the heavens, but because of what she could do to them. Being a succubus certainly has its advantages, but right now, with no guy to woo she was in the same situation as Molly and myself.

"Will you two be quiet? I can't afford to go to detention again." My voice hissed as I glared at them.

"If we get caught, it won't be because of us." Molly hissed right back at me as she crossed her arms against her chest. Damn, the girl tried to be intimidating with her eyebrow arched, but with her button nose and pale fairy skin she just couldn't pull it off.

"Right," I said turning back to scan the chain linked fence that separated our world from the humans. It was so close, the sight and smell of salty bodies and drumming heart beats that I could almost reach out and take them. The only problem was the field of harpies perched along the scare crows waiting to sound the alarm.

"What are you waiting for?" Shannon asked nudging her shoulder into my back. "Just do it already so we can get out of here."

I sucked in a deep breath allowing the air to fill my lungs to the point of popping. Just as the last inch of space was filled in my chest with air I held it. My lungs longed for the release, but I wasn't ready to give in, not yet. I loved depriving myself of such basic needs. It thrilled me to know I was in control of my body even if I wasn't in control of anything else.

Slowly I let the air whiz out of my lips. Little by little the burning sensation ceased only to be replaced by a longing and need to fill back up again. I collapsed my lungs and drained them of all oxygen before pulling in another breath. It was the longing, the deep yearning and pleasure of denying myself of the basic need to breathe that would spark the flame within me. Only when the rubber band expanded to the point of breaking would my Valkyrie side come out. Casting was hard enough without having stage fright, yet the pressure to perform rattled my nerves.

Granted it was my first time pulling off such a feat, I wasn't certain the hideous half bird half hags would be effected. It was that fear, that uncertainty I was trying to drain out of me as I rolled my shoulders back and concentrated on their beaded little heads and plump feathered bodies.

Shit, what the hell is that? The icy grip of death stole the warmth of me as every fiber in my body went hollow. Death pulled me into its frigid embrace like a welcoming lover. The color of the world vanished from my eyes as I glared at the ragged little puff balls on their perfect little perches. A smile crept over my lips as my shadow slithered out before me inching itself closer to the wards of the Draconian Academy.

The harpies in all their hideous gory details squawked and clamored about until my shadow kissed each one dropping them like flies.

"You're doing it, Kira," cooed Molly as the beating of her wings filled my ears with their incessant humming. Carefully I pulled my shadow back absorbing the darkness into me. My ears popped as if I dove into a deep abyss with the weight of gravity crushing down on me before the soft blue sky and crisp green grass returned.

"Come on," Molly giggled as she stepped past me into the field. My heart slowed as I took in all the harpies twitching on the ground at my feet. Pride swelled in my very soul as Shannon rapped her hand on my shoulder.

"Not bad," she complemented as the soft grass crunched under her foot. It was just a few yards to the fence. A quick sprint and we would make it to the other side. Electricity coursed through me as I watched Shannon and Molly frolic through the field inching their way closer to the border.

"What the hell do you think you girls are doing?" The three of us frozen in our tracks. No one dared to glimpse over our shoulders as the voice boomed in over our heads.

"Retract your steps."

Oh shit, here came the voice of reason, the sergeant of pain and torment himself. I was the first to turn. With my heart rattling in my chest, the sound filling my ears with ever beat, and the pulse of light flashing through my eyes as I turned to face him.

"Hello Max." Blood surged to my head as I laid eyes on him. It was his silky smooth baritone voice that drew me to him. Never mind his golden locks and caramel eyes surged with a rage only an Ares could conjure.

"What did you do to these poor things?" He asked turning his attention to the heap of bodies dropped by my shadow. I shrugged as I blushed unapologetically.

"Shannon, Molly," Max growled flashing his eyes in their direction. Before Max could distribute his wrath, they were gone.

Some friends. I lifted my hand up shielding my eyes from the glare of the sun as they vanished.

"Looks like you and I have a date," Max said as his eyes narrowed in on me.

"You know I loved our time together, but I really think you should get over me," I teased as I moved closer to him. My fingertips burned as I grazed over his chest and batted my eyes. Even the slightest touch caused his body to quiver. His eyes rolled as his lips thinned into a tight line.

"Funny, and here I thought you were trying to escape this route to get my attention."

I glared at him. His words weren't completely false. But I wasn't about to let him know that. By the flash of rage in his eyes he already had his mind made up about what I was doing at this particular exit.

"You know, you could just look the other way and say you never saw us," I said smoothing out the wrinkles of his blue buttoned down shirt with my finger. His hand whipped up and grabbed mine.

Damn did I love his touch, if it wasn't for his obsessiveness we could have really been something. Still, he was who he was and there was no changing a demi-god's mind once it was set. I jerked my hand out of his.

"Not going to happen this time." Max's voice growled as he leaned closer to me. His hot breath caressed my cheeks sending shivers flowing down my spine. If it wasn't for the fact he broke up with me, this conversation would be going in completely different direction.

"Detention. Now."

"Come on," I stepped back trying to cool the flames he fanned in me.

"Your tricks don't work on me anymore."

"Sure they do," I countered.

"I'm serious Kira."

"So am I." To my surprise my voice cooed as I answered him. His fingers curled around my arm as he pulled me back to the stone buildings.

"Detention."

"Fine," I growled as I kept my eyes locked on him. His caramel colored hair lightened in the light of the sun as the wind played with it. His dark eyes grew faint and shifted into the icy blue I loved so much the closer we got to the school.

Of course, he didn't want to scare the other students by his placid eyes that drew souls into the abyss. I however was never frightened by the darkness I found in them. Yet, I knew he'd have to change his eye color much to my dismay.

A giggle slipped from my lips as the lights flickered above our heads.

"What?" he glanced down at me.

I shook my head holding back from laughing at the eyeballs on us as we marched down the hall. For a moment I wondered if they were concerned for my safety. After all, they heard the rumors of his powers. Yet, no one, save a selected few actually saw them. I, of course saw him in all his raging glory. It was that fierceness and strength that first drew me to him. Even now as he dragged me through the hallway towards the last classroom, I saw a sliver of his might and felt my body ache for him.

"Get in there," he ordered as the door flew open. He tossed me into the empty room and closed the door behind us.

"I remember this place," I said tiptoeing around the desks as I ran my fingers over the coarse wooden tables.

"Kira, this is detention."

"Do you remember when I came to you in here three years ago? You weren't the head security back then." The thought of his bare chest pressed against mine as our lips parted one another's thrilled me. A giggle slipped as the memory of our bodies entwined in a heated mess on the newly waxed floor played at the fringes of my mind.

"Now look at you," I spun around to take a step away from him only to have his hands hold me fast. Max grabbed my hips holding me in place. His chest rose and fell rapidly and I couldn't help but lick the rim of my lips teasing him.

"Kira," his voice was frail, barely a whisper. Lifting my leg I ran my knee over his inner thigh and up to his groin. A pulse against my knee said more than he could ever express. His fingers tightened around my hips as my fingers drifted over the buttons of his shirt and slipped further down. The smooth fabric of his slacks tickled my fingertips.

Please tell me you want me.

My heart raced as I drifted further south. *Just three tiny inches of zipper.* Holding his gaze I pinched the cold metal clasp. The ripping of metal as the zipper dropped filled my ears. By the spark in his eyes he heard it too. Carefully I slipped my fingers through the small hole to graze his flesh.

"I do miss you," I confessed leaning closer to him. The heat of his body singed my torso as I wrapped my free arm around his neck. "I miss the things you used to do to me." If there was one thing I was a master of, it was the tease.

Please take me right here, like we've done so many times before. My breath was quick as the thoughts filled my mind of everything I wanted to do to him.

"You're lying."

"I'm not," through the veil of my eyelids I glanced up to him. God why did he have to be so irresistible? Why did I have to be so greedy? My body trembled under his firm grip as my lips brushed against his ear.

"Take me. Right here."

The grip around my hips tightened as his chest rose and fell. His hot breath caressed my lips as I watched the torment in his eyes.

The buzzing of the bell intruded and pulled me out of my need for him. Reality sucked, and we both knew it. As my fingers inched down his hard smooth shaft I panted.

Damn it to hell. I nibbled on my lower lip and held him a brief moment more wishing for once he would take the lead. But he remained so still so calm I couldn't help but smile. He was trying to control his appetite.

"Maybe next time," I said as I slipped my hand out of his pants and pecked him hard on the cheek. Soon the hallways would be clamored with students. The last thing we wanted was to be spotted like this, a student and professor. Although, everyone knew we were an item at one point. But in order for him to get his promotion, he had to ditch dating the students. That included me.

"It's always a pleasure," I said pushing away. My body trembled as I pushed down the flames. My body ached for him and for a moment I wondered if he missed me too.

Swallowing hard, I wiggled out of his embrace and smiled.

"Maybe we can pick up later?" He asked releasing me.

"What about your position? Won't that compromise you?" My eyes darted to his trousers as his crotch twitched.

"I'll deal with that later."

"Sorry, but Luke is probably waiting for me," I said flipping my locks over my shoulder as I trotted to the door.

"You're still with him?" Max's voice ached catching me off guard. I glanced over my shoulder flashing a wicked little grin.

"That's really none of your business anymore. You left me remember?"

"But Luke? That scrawny kid who doesn't know how to handle you? Please, you must be joking."

"Actually, I believe it was you who can't handle me." *Wink. That will throw him for a loop.*

I batted my eyes and turned my attention to the door. Reaching out I turned the knob to let the sounds fill the classroom. The instant I pulled the door open, a whiff of sulfur assaulted my nose. I turned only to find Max gone, all that remained was the puff of smoke lingering in the air where he once stood.

"Oh Max," I whispered as I walked through the door. The sounds of laughter and chatted filled my ears as I pulled down the fabric of my skirt as eyes flickered to me. I was greeted with a spark of curiosity and jealousy. If only they knew. I chuckled as I walked towards the cafeteria hoping Shannon and Molly would be there. If not, there was always the library.

Chapter 2

"So, Kira," Shannon giggled as her eyebrows wiggled. "How was detention?"

"You know I would never kiss and tell." The urge to keep my private moments with Max was unbearable. Of course I would tell my two best friends - eventually. But for now, I enjoyed the way they squirmed in their seats itching for some juicy tidbits.

Molly's shoulders slumped as her face dropped in complete discouragement, " Oh come on, just a little something? Did he spank you like he did last time?"

"It wasn't like that." I tried to keep from sighing. Zeus knows I would have loved for it to be that way. Yet, he wasn't playing my game. At least not right now. A flicker of a smile escaped my lips causing Shannon and Molly to jolt up.

"Sure it wasn't." *Ah, Shannon always the reasonable one. Of course she could see my aura pulsing and pick up everything she wanted to know just by looking at me.* Luckily though, she couldn't read my mind and couldn't see the details, only imagine what took place.

"See, it's goes around and then up." The low rumble of his voice caught me off guard. I turned my head to spot Luke walking alongside his friends. The hardy boys as I liked to call them. Not because they were rough or anything, but because of who their parents were.

Luke, my flavor of the month happened to be Apollo's son. He had the dreamiest eyes, soft like the twinkling of stars. He was kind and gentle, a trait that seemed to pass Max by completely. And when he looked at me, my heart fluttered.

"Easy there tiger," Shannon whispered in my ear. I could only imagine the shift of colors in my aura as I spotted Luke.

His eyes darted my way and held my gaze. I didn't care that Chase, Poseidon's son was there with his dark hair and eyes like the sea after a storm. Even he was swoon worthy. But it was Luke who I couldn't take my eyes off of.

Come hither, please.

As if answering my inner desires Luke waved off his friends and made his rounds to me. My heart fluttered with every step he took. Before I could say hi, his hands were around my waist pulling me to him. His tender lips parted mine and stole the breath out of me.

"Hello beautiful." He pulled away and flashed his brilliant smile that caused my head to spin.

"Luke." I swallowed trying hard to keep myself in check. But the longer I stared at him, the further away everyone else appeared to me. Even Shannon and Molly faded into the back ground as my body trembled under his touch. It was Max's fault I felt so needed. After all, it was Max who got me all hot and bothered only to leave in a puff a smoke once the bell rang.

"So," I glanced up to Luke and traced my fingers gingerly up his chest. "What are you up to?"

"It depends." Man how I hated when he teased me. The sparkle in his eyes lured me in and all I wanted was to find some secret room to be alone with him.

"We were trying to ditch earlier. Maybe we can give it another go?" Molly suggested. Her voice was like nails on a chalk board breaking through my twisted fantasy of fucking Luke in the broom closet.

"Sorry, but I don't think Max will be so forgiving to me," Luke said with a wink.

"You heard about that huh?" My face burned hotter as I tucked a strand of hair behind my ear.

"As soon as the bell rang, he was at my class giving me the third degree."

So that's where Max went in such a hurry.

"But since when do I listen to him?" Luke winked as he snuggled me closer. Suddenly I could feel a ray of heat cutting into my spine. I didn't have to turn around to know Max was in the cafeteria with us. No doubt watching my interactions with Luke.

Good. I hope you like what you see.

I turned my head and winked at Max standing in the corner with his arms crossed and face red. He was pissed, no doubt about that. But I didn't care. He should have taken me when we had the chance.

"What do you say, Luke?" I reached up to my tiptoes and leaned my whole body into him. My hot breath tickled his ear as I spoke,"Wanna find some place a little less crowded?"

"Sounds like fun."

"But?"

"Is Luke afraid of big old Max?" Shannon giggled as Molly laughed too. I whipped my head to my friends and pulled away from Luke.

"It's okay Luke," Shannon said stepping closer to him. She ran her fingers down his chest. My eyes lit up as I watched her body flow with a golden glow, like a gentle current of water glistening in the sun light. Luke shivered as she worked her magic on him.

"You don't need to worry about Max," Shannon said as Molly cupped her hand over her mouth and shook her head. Luke's eyes fluttered at Shannon's touch. Jealousy coursed through me as I watched how easily Luke was persuaded by Shannon.

Man how I wish I could do that. But then again… My eyes flickered to Shannon. She was trembling as dirty little thoughts filled her mind. Her lips parted into a gentle "O" as she shuttered. Luke moaned and quivered as his hands dropped from my hips to the table to support himself.

"Well," I said stepping back. "Don't mind me."

"I don't think they were," Molly said as Shannon released Luke. I shook my head and crossed my arms over my chest as Luke's eyes fluttered open. His mouth was parched as his attention flickered to Shannon.

"I really hate it when you do that. It is such a tease," he grumbled as Shannon stepped back from the table. Her cheeks flushed red as I turned my eyes to Max in the corner. My favorite smile lingered on his lips.

Damn it, he was watching the whole thing.

Irritation and jealousy coursed through me. I wanted that release. Luke leaned down and curled his arms around my neck. His lips pressed against my neck.

"Tonight," he promised. "If you don't have other plans."

"Didn't you get enough with Shannon?" I couldn't help but let the bitterness seep through.

"Please, all I did was tease him," Shannon admitted. "He didn't even blow his load, look."

My eyes flickered to Luke's pants expecting to find a wet spot around his crotch. But the dry fabric shocked me. I wasn't expecting him to hold out. No one ever held out to Shannon.

"Only you Babe," he whispered. "Tonight. After this. I really need you."

A sense of fulfillment and power surged through me. Of course he would wait for me. Feeling a bit stupid and insecure I nodded and threw my arms around his neck.

"Tonight. I promise."

"Don't let Max know." Luke's eyes flickered to Max and I couldn't help but follow them. Max was not in the happiest of moods. His face was stern and his muscles taught. I wondered if he would burn the whole place down.

Molly giggled as the bell rang. Luke released me and I suddenly felt cold. With a brush of his hand over my cheek he puckered his lips and blew me a kiss.

"Gotta go hot stuff. But I'm going to hold you to your word."

"Tonight. At the bleachers. When the moon is high."

"What is it with you and the bleachers?" Molly asked shaking her head. "Not everyone wants to see you doing it."

"Yes they do," Luke answered as he turned. "Or haven't you seen a Valkyrie getting her grove on?"

Molly's eyebrows crunched into her brow as she cocked her head. Luke was slipping through the aisle of the tables as the cafeteria emptied. I couldn't help but feel a flutter of butterflies in my stomach as I watched him walk away.

"You know you can't keep stringing both of them along right?" Shannon said as she scooped her arm around mine. Molly stood and moved to Shannon's other side as the three of us mozied out of the cafeteria.

"Why not? They both know what they were getting themselves into when they picked me. If they want a girlfriend, they are going to have to get that from someone else.”

Seriously? What kind of guilt trip was Shannon was giving me? I glanced at her through the corner of my eye double checking to see if she was projecting any negative feelings on to me. To my surprise she wasn’t. It was just Shannon, being the kind hearted succubus she always was.

“I can see what you are doing to them.” Shannon said as she sighed. “Yet, you know Max can’t stand Luke.”

“That’s Max’s problem. But as for Luke, he doesn’t mind.” I shrugged as we walked down the hallway. Students and faculty raced to get to their next classes. I couldn’t care if I arrived on time or not. The only reason I came to this stupid school was because I needed to learn control of my casting. Everything else was a joke. But still, there was Molly and Shannon who took their studies seriously. At least, they seemed to.

“That’s because Luke is an air head and you know it.” Molly interjected. “That boy will do anything you want. All you got to say is the word.”

“But that’s why I love him so.”

“Love?” Shannon came to an abrupt stop and glanced over to me. Her eyes were filled with wonder and awe as she shook her head. "Did the word love actually escape your lips?"

"You know what I mean," I pulled my arm out of hers and pressed my lips into a tight line. My eyes narrowed. She couldn't be serious. Yet, the expression of shock never left her face.

"Why can't you love one and let the other go?" asked Shannon.

"Valkyries don't love. You both know that."

"Oh don't give me that horse shit," Shannon huffed as Molly crossed her arms over her chest mimicking Shannon. "Alexandra found love."

"Alexandra is an idiot."

Molly cocked her head as a somber expression drifted over her face. "But why? Because she found love? Love is the most powerful force of all. It can make you do crazy things and mend all wounds. It is the source of everything." Molly's face lit up with such a light I had to shield my eyes from her glow.

"I just can't stand the thought of losing someone that I would love. I know where people go after they die. I know what happens to them. I could never imagine having to carry their soul to the other side and be like. Whoops sorry, you did wrong so yeah bye."

Fear and angst filled my heart as I thought about it. I knew there was no telling exactly where a soul went, but still I would be one of many to deliver it there. *And then what? Say a long hard goodbye? No thank you.*

"So that's why you only go after demi-gods, huh? Because they are immortal?" Shannon's voice was faint.

"I don't have to say goodbye to them. And our flirting and spontaneous time together doesn't mean anything in the scope of forever. I get all the good stuff and none of the bad. As long as everyone understands that we don't commit."

"You know Max would have, if you would have asked," Shannon said as the last bit of students rushed into their classes.

"He did ask, I said no."

"One of these days you'll find someone who is going to make you change your mind about love."

"And when that day comes I promise, I'll give up Max and Luke. But until then. I'm going to have my cake and eat it too."

Chapter 3

A chill raced down my spine and like talons of a griffin digging into its prey, my heart froze. The hallway of the school swayed as my head spun.

Shit. Not now. Not here.

I pulled in deep frantic breaths trying to steady my nerves as the beams of light flickered. Blinking I tried to keep my head on straight. I tried to focus on Shannon and Molly. But it was no use. I was being summoned. The cry of the Valkyrie penetrated every fiber of my being and stealing the very warmth of my body. All the passion I felt for Luke vanished as if someone poured icy cold water over my head and drenched me.

"Step back." Molly's voice cried out as the skin under my shoulder blades split open releasing the wings of an angel. I glanced up as each beat of my heart thundered in my ears. The tunnel of white, glorious light opened above my head and I knew where the light would take me.

Closing my eyes I let the light consume me. It caressed every inch of my skin bring warmth back into me. Every beam of light, every crackle of energy that pricked my skin pulled me up. I opened my wings as the image of a woman came into my head. There she was, the slain looking porcelain doll. She remained unmoving, unloving as her brown hair clung to her neck like seaweed. I swallowed hard forcing the air down as I rose up. Each beat of my wings drew me to her as the light engulfed me in its warmth.

"Kira." My voice was too far away, too faint for me to pay any mind to. It was as if a dream called out to me and before I could snap out of it, I was gone. The light circled me and pulled me, kissed me and drained me. Every bit of my body trembled with excitement. The higher I climbed the harder it was for me to focus on anything other than the beautiful girl with dark hair. She fought well. She was a warrior worth going to.

I sucked in a deep breath and reached my arm out to her trying to pull her image closer to me. The light singed my eyes as I passed the through the tunnel drawing ever closer to the woman stained with blood.

Death was a beautiful thing. A peaceful emotion that overcame all of my emotions. It was stronger than love. Stronger than life. It was the epitome of and the finale of the universe. So many people wondered where the universe began and where it ended. For me, it was in the glassy eyes of a warrior I was summoned to collect. It was my life's purpose to meet the fallen in the light and bring them to the other side.

Luckily for me, this woman Valerie was decent. She wasn't going to the darker side of the universe. Her soul was engulfed in the light and flowed freely up to me as I hovered above her body.

The clashing of metal on metal caught my attention. The battle cries of days of old surrounded me. No longer could I keep my focus on the woman with pale skin and dark hair.

No. I was drawn to something else. Someone else. There through the beams of light and rainbows I saw him. The mortal - thrashing his arms about as he defended the woman's body.

"My son." Her voice was but a whisper, a hint of a sound through the crackles and flickers of energy that surrounded us. I drifted my eyes to her. It was the pride in her face, the love in her eyes, the sadness in her stance that haunts me.

"It is your time," I said holding out my hand to her.

Please just take my hand. I have but one job to do and you are making it so difficult. But the woman shook her head and pointed to her son wielding the frying pan like a sword as he defended against the onslaught of the dark fae.

"Please," she pleaded refusing my hand. "He must not be killed."

"That is not for you to decide."

She cocked her head as her eyes lingered on me as if she knew precisely what I was. "No, but you can."

It was true, a Valkyrie had the power to sway the battle to one side or another. But he was a mortal against fae. A human battling for a body whose soul was already passing through to Valhalla's gates. I stopped and studied him.

Sweat dripped down his brow as his muscles tightened with each blow. He fought like a champion of old. Yet, he was human.

How is this possible?

There was no denying that he was a might soldier up against great odds. But I was not called to humans very often. My eyes darted to the woman, and I gasped. She did not have the glow of the fae. She did not have the fragrance of tube rose but that of honey. She too once was mortal, and yet I was called to her.

"Who are you?" I demanded stepping back into the light daring to leave her soul where it stayed.

"I'm no one. But that boy is my son. Please, you must help him."

As I lingered in the veil between worlds, I watched him fly back into the wall as the three dark fae moved in on him. He was out numbered, out powered, and still he rose to the occasion. Watching him hold out and hold on thrilled me. My heart fluttered wondering if he would scramble to his feet and continue or if he was spent.

To my utter amazement he rose once more to his feet, his eyes narrowed as determination settled on his features. A smile played at the corner of his lips as if to taught his assailants. It was there at that moment I understood. My heart dropped as my hands grew sweaty.

Breaking through the veil, I cast my shadow out into the room and with a loud voice shouted, "Enough."

The dark faes vanished from the room as the human crumbled in the corner weeping. As my foot touched down on the plush carpet, I stared at him. After all, he had done to fend off such creatures I was who he feared?

"What is your name?" I demanded as my shadow kissed and caressed every inch of the room pulling all light out of the world. The boy quaked in the corner as tears poured from his eyes.

"Brandon."

"Your mother is dead and yet you defend her why?"

"She was all I had left."

"You did not fight like someone who wished to join her," I said lifting my sight up to the tunnel. The dark haired beauty peered down at us, her eyebrows pulled together as she blew kisses his way.

"I don't…" He paused and dropped his hand. Brandon's eyes gaze was not that of pity or sorrow, but of hope. "What are you?"

"That's not polite to ask," I said shaking my head.

Well shit. Now I've done it. Okay think. Do I a) wipe his memory of meeting me? I mean he is human after all. Or b)kill him and take him with us to the other side? I glared at him as he rose to his feet and dropped the frying pan.

"What were those things?" Glancing around his place he seemed to have put up quite a fight. Dishes lay broken on the ground. Food splattered across the back of the stove. Burned marking singed the walls and a distinct odor of moss and muck lingered on the air.

"From the damage I think they were furies."

"Wait what? You mean like Greek mythology?"

"I don't know about mythology, but most do hail from Greece. And most are super nasty and vengeful."

Damn it Kira shut up before you end up telling too much. I pressed my lips into a tight line as I tried not to kick myself too much. One more rookie mistake and I'm never going to graduate. I exhaled slowly as I studied him. He knew too much, saw too much, and experienced far too much.

"I'm sorry," I whispered as I focused all my energy on him. He stared at me with his deep green eyes that reminded me of the green fields of Ireland. They weren't quite emerald, but stark and beautiful. I tried to pull the memories from his mind and dig out the events. But no matter how deep I penetrated his mind, I could barely scratch the surface.

I pulled back panting and heaving as he stood unaffected. He glanced around confused. I moved forward and placed my hands on his shoulders.

"What are you doing?"

"You. Have. To. Forget."

I panted and heaved. Every muscle in my body ached as my wings clenched to my body as I concentrated. For a moment I wondered if he thought I was constipated, after all that's how I felt at the moment. Clogged and unmoving.

After several attempts I backed away. Sweat dripped from my forehead and down to my temples. Quickly I wiped it off and rubbed the back of my neck. There was only one other person who could fend off my advance. My eyes narrowed as I glared at him. No flashing flames or brimstone buried in his gaze. He was human, yet he held me back.

"Brandon. Here's the thing. You know too much. You've seen too much. And frankly I have told you too much. I can't wipe your mind of these memories…" I panted trying to catch my breath as I talked. "And since I can't. I'm going to have to kill you."

"What?!"

"It's okay. Your mom is waiting for you. A little nick on the neck and it'll be over quickly." He stepped back with his hands up. For a moment he looked more scared of what I suggested than what he just witnessed.

"You can't do that."

"Actually I can. It's kind of what I do. There's a reason Valkyries are known as angels of death."

"No. I'm not going to die today." He dropped to the ground and grabbed the frying pan once again. Brandon swung the metal plate out before him trying to force me back.

A chuckled escaped my lips, "You're joking right?"

"Stay back. I took out those other things, I can take you out too."

"No. You can't." I pushed my shadow out and blanketed his body. Through my shadow I felt every pain, every joy, every excitement that washed through him. He was more than terrified, he was eager. I could taste it on my lips and smell the sweat fragrance of honeysuckle.

Stepping towards him, he swung the pan back and released. The crack of the pan against the side of my head rumbled the windows. I glared at him unmoved by his foolish attempt.

"Please," he resorted to begging as he dropped the pan once more. "I don't want to die. Take me with you."

"You don't know where I am going."

"I don't care. Any place is better than here. I mean look around. My mom's is gone. The house is wrecked and chances are the cops will think I did all this. But if I'm gone too. Then at least I'll have a shot ya know?"

"Tell me Brandon, who was it that attacked you?"

"I don't know. Honestly I don't. My mom was just cooking in the kitchen and the next thing I know she's dead, and those things were all over me."

"Why?"

"Beats me, but don't you think that's worth letting me tag along? I mean maybe we can figure that out."

I pulled in a deep slow breath as he cupped his hands together. He did after all battle three furies and live. Maybe there was something more to him than meets the eyes.

"Fine. You can come with. But no long good byes with your mother. The guardians don't like it when there is a soul with spirit if you know what I mean."

"Seriously?" My eyebrow rose with irritation as I reached out a hand to him.

"Awesome."

"I mean what I said about long goodbyes. Keep it short got it?" He nodded once as I pulled my shadow to me and let the light return to the world. His eyes grew wider as he gazed at me.

"What?" I asked, my eyes narrowing in on him.

"You are beautiful," he choked.

"Yeah, I get that a lot."

"No, I mean like…" he didn't finish, his eyes flickered around my face and body as his mouth popped open.

"I never knew angels existed. But now, wow."

"Sorry but I don't date humans. Too short a life span," I said pulling him closer to me and rose up into the tunnel of light.

Chapter 4

"What the hell are you doing bringing him here?" Molly's eyes widened. I glanced to Shannon. Her eyes sparkled, and she stared at the human by my side.

"I had no other choice."

"You could have left him where ever you found him," Molly hissed stepping back from Brandon. Her wings fluttered frantically lifting her feet off the ground. Brandon shook his eyes as his mouth dropped.

"Where am I? This can't be real. Am I," he swallowed hard as fear washed over his face. "Dead?"

Shannon's laughter trickled out breaking the tension. "No, would you like to be? I can give you the most sensational death you could ever dream." Shannon lifted her hand and wiggled her fingers, tempting Brandon to touch her. A smile played at the corner of my lips as I wondered if he would take the bait.

Hesitating he stepped closer to Shannon and grazed his fingers over Shannon's. Half amused my eyes flickered to his crotch. The metal zipper of his pants twitched as his cock grew thicker. For a moment I wondered what fantastic things Shannon was showing him, what pleasures she infused into him.

"Alright, you've had your fun," I snapped as Brandon's knees buckled from under him. Shannon dropped her hand as Brandon gasped for air. He looked up at Shannon with wild, hungry eyes.

"Please, more," he pleaded as he wobbled to touch her again.

"Sorry human, anymore and you'll be out like yesterday's garbage. And truth be told, I don't want to have to hide a body today. I've got other plans." Shannon flipped her hair over her shoulder as she glanced to Molly.

"Come on, let's leave Kira with her new friend."

"But…" Brandon started as his eyes darted to me.

"And for the record ladies," I threw my hands to my hips and glared at them. I could feel my shadow begging to be unleashed as the irritation rose in me. "I don't date humans."

"Sure you don't," Shannon winked as she curled her arm around Molly. I shook my head as Molly and Shannon disappeared in a resounding crack leaving me alone in the abandoned classroom with the human.

"Seriously, what is this place?" Brandon asked as his eyes flickered from one corner of the room to the next. I stepped back and exhaled slowly.

"Welcome to Tartarus High," I lifted my arms up and spun around.

"This isn't the real world is it?" he asked stepping to the window of the empty class room.

"It's as real as where you come from. You could say it is on the other side of the veil."

"The veil?"

I stepped to the window next to him and pointed towards the chain linked fence. A part of me shuttered to spot the harpies resting back on their perches so soon. But that was to be expected.

"Do you see the shimmer past the fence? That rainbow shimmer playing with the sun light?" I asked pointing over the field. Brandon squinted his eyes as he stepped closer to me. His head bobbed and for the first time I could smell the strong ivory scent drifting off his skin.

The aroma pulled me like a honey bee. All I wanted to do was merge into him and have his body fill me up. I shook my head trying to surface from the fantasy and cleared my throat.

"That is the veil," I said as I caught him staring at me in the corner of my eye. "It's the border of our reality and yours."

"So…" he leaned closer to the glass as I stepped away. "I can leave at any time just by walking through that veil?"

"Sort of. You kind of need a fae to help you out with that. Although…" I wondered what would happen to a human trying to cross the realms. It had never been done before without the help of a fae. There weren't any stories of such things happening. Then again, how many times had a human been brought to our side.

I shrugged and forced myself to smile as I turned to face him. "You could try. But I doubt you'll get past the harpies. Those bitches are a pain in anyone's ass."

"Real harpies? Like from Greek mythology?"

"I don't know what you're talking about." My eyebrow rose as I stared at him.

Humans, of course they would think our kind was make believe. How else could they sleep at night?

"Never mind," Brandon said shrugging. He flashed a smile that lit up the room as he rubbed his hands together. "Can you show me more?"

"As long as you keep your eyes down. I don't need you to draw attention to yourself here, got it?"

"Of course. I'll do whatever you say. Just, I can't believe it ya know?"

Dread filled the core of my stomach as I glanced at him. I turned and walked to the door and pulled it open slowly. I could feel his hot breath on my neck as I peeked out of the doorway. The hallway was nearly empty only a few students lingered about. By the light of the sun blazing through the windows there was no doubt classes were adjourned.

Yes. This will be easier than I thought.

I pulled open the door and stepped out into the hallway with Brandon at my side. We strolled through the hallway, my shoes clapping the tile as we moved.

"Try not to stare," I reminded Brandon as his mouth dropped open. Of course he'd find the nymphs gorgeous, most of the guys did. I shook my head and kept moving hoping to make it down the hallway before we could be spotted by anyone important. The last thing I wanted was to come face to face with Max right now. He wouldn't hesitate to bring down fire and brimstone.

"Kira?" My heart dropped. Of course it would be him. Brandon turned first as I stood still praying I had the ability to go invisible.

"Hey Luke," I finally said turning. His bright smile and warmth soothed my fears. He was the one person I should have known wouldn't care if a human was here.

Luke's eyes dazzled over Brandon for a moment before returning to me. "Who's your friend? Molly and Shannon said he was a human, but I didn't believe them."

"Luke, this Brandon. Brandon this is my…" Well, I honestly didn't know what Luke was. He wasn't a boyfriend. We hadn't made it to that point, and I didn't want to. But he was more than just a friend.

"I'm one of her toys," Luke answered. I choked on a laugh as Luke spoke. That was a perfect example of what he was. Brandon's eyes flickered to me as he crossed his arms over his chest. Confusion drifted over his features.

"Toy?" Brandon cleared his throat as a spark of recognition flashed in his eyes. His mouth drew open to an "o" shape as he nodded. "Friends with benefits. I gotcha."

"Sure, whatever," I said trying not to let the flush of embarrassment show.

"You know Kira, there are some people here that won't be too happy you bringing a human to the party,"

Luke said keeping his eyes locked on Brandon. I reached for the human and curled my fingers around his arm holding Brandon closer.

"You aren't going to say anything are you? I mean he is only here until I can figure out who killed his mother."

"Why should the death of a human matter to you?" Luke's eyebrow in suspicion.

"I was called to collect his mother earlier," I confessed. Luke's eyes widened as he wrapped his head around what I said.

"You're joking right? A human? But you are only called to our kind."

"That's what I thought too. But apparently I'm not. So here we are. Now there were dark fae involved. Three furies attacked him and his mother."

"Furies?" Luke rubbed his chin as he glanced over my shoulder as if lost in a deep thought.

"There are only a handful of people who have contact with the furies," Luke said.

My heart sank. *Please don't say Max. Please. Please. Please.*

"You'll have to talk to Max about that."

"You know how he feels about humans," I said flashing my eyes to Brandon.

"Kira, may I have a word alone?" Luke asked as he reached out for my arm. I slipped my hand off Brandon and nodded. There was something in his tone that threw me off. A warning of sorts that dug under my skin and pulled me towards him.

I flashed a quick smile to Brandon as I stepped away with Luke. Gripping my arm he led me around the corner and pressed me against the wall. His warm body against mine set my desires ablaze.

Don't look in his eyes, don't look in his eyes. But I couldn't help it. Not with him stroking the back of his fingers over my cheek. I closed my eyes and allowed myself to be pulled into his touch. Nothing mattered. Brandon and his troubles, Max and his jealousy. It was only me here in this moment with Luke.

"Kira, what are you doing with the human?" he asked. His breath tickled my ear as he spoke soothingly to me.

"I have to help him."

"Are you sure that it all there is to this union?" he asked as his fingertips returned to my cheek.

"Yes." My heart sank to my stomach as butterflies took flight causing chaos within me.

"You seem attached to him."

"Impossible. Humans are too weak for our kind. They couldn't handle this life."

"I just needed to be sure of your intentions with him," Luke said brushing his lips over my neck as he nibbled down to my shoulder. Each kiss sent chills through me. It was as if I stepped into the sun itself only to be pulled back into shadow each time his lips left my skin.

"It's just you," I promised.

"And Max." He reminded me.

I couldn't deny that. Max was still a part of my life whether I wanted him or not. But my heart teetered more to Luke than anyone else.

"Only a tiny bit," I lifted my hand up to show only a centimeter of space between my finger and my thumb. Luke's hand grazed down my chest as his eyes locked me in place.

His fingertips warmed and stroked my desires until he found the hem of my skirt and played under the heavy fabric.

"You promised we'd play later today remember?"

"I haven't forgotten. When the moon is high, I'll meet you under the bleachers."

"Good," Luke said stepping away. I could barely breathe. My body was a jumbled mess as I came out of the daze. My eyes darted around trying to remember where I was. Luke certainly left me with a lasting impression as I watched him drift down the hallway and disappear around the corner.

Get it together. Breathe. I pulled in a deep gulp of air as I heard Shannon's muffled laughter around the corner. I glanced over my shoulder as a distinct sickness turned my stomach.

Oh shit. Brandon.

Chapter 5

Pulling my shirt down I tried to compose myself as I stepped around the corner only to be greeted by the empty hallway. My eyes darted to and fro searching relentlessly for Brandon. With my stomach in knots my ears perked to Shannon's soft giggles.

Step by step I followed the muffled sounds and paused at the broom closet in the center of the hallway. My eyes shifted to the left and right before I reached out with a trembling hand to the doorknob. With a sudden jerk I pulled open the door.

My mouth dropped as did my heart as a blueish glow drifted out of Brandon's mouth and into Shannon's. The smile on Brandon's face reminded me of how goofy I must look to Max or Luke when I get weak in the knees. Jealousy boiled in me causing my blood to run icy as I reached out and tapped Shannon on the shoulder.

"What is this?" I demanded as she released Brandon from her succubus kiss. She batted her eyes as she turned to me innocently.

"What? You didn't think you could just keep him to yourself did you?"

"You could have killed him," I said pushing her to the side as I scooped Brandon into my arms and pulled him out of the corner of the broom closet.

"Please, just because you can't control your thing doesn't mean the rest of us can't. Beside," Shannon's eyes flickered to Brandon as a wicked and mischievous smile pulled at the corners of her lips. "He liked it."

"No duh. But he is human," I hissed hoisting Brandon to his feet as he mumbled gibberish to me. Studying him, my mouth dropped. He wasn't completely incoherent. His eyes were still focused and his face still had color to it. Even the strongest human couldn't have lasted ten seconds with Shannon. I whipped my attention to Shannon. She stepped around me with her judgmental eyes narrowing in on me.

"Maybe he isn't what you thought he was," she said as she shoved her shoulder into mine.

"He certainly doesn't taste human."

"But that's not possible." My voice was no more than a whisper as confusion stepped in. Brandon smiled at me deliriously as I propped him up against the wall. His head bobbled and swayed as his eyes swam in euphoria.

"Are you okay?" I asked him slapping my palm to his face.

"Never better," he answered trying to focus. Irritation boiled to the surface as I slammed his body against the wall.

"She could have killed you. Do you understand that? There are fae here that won't hesitate or restrain themselves."

"But she was so good," Brandon cooed as I turned to look at Shannon. Her smile stretched further over her face as she admired her nails and shrugged obviously pleased with herself.

"See, no harm done."

"He is practically a zombie," I said trying not to knock Brandon around as my frustrations grew.

"You have those here?" Brandon's eyes widened as they scanned the hallway searching for the unseen threat.

"Looks like lover boy here needs some shut eye," Shannon said as her eyebrow arched.

"What are you going on about?" I didn't want to hear Shannon's voice any more, but by the spark in her eyes and the self-confident stance she had, I knew she had answers. Maybe even clues as to who attacked him earlier.

"He's in love. Lovers always have a special kind of taste to them," she said winking at me.

"That's because you put those thoughts into him." I dropped my shoulders and let Brandon slip from my grasp. He slumped to the ground and hummed to himself. I shook my head and stepped back from him as I turned to Shannon.

"Did you get anything from him?"

"I got a lot from him sugar. What are you wanting to know?" Shannon smirked as she plucked the dirt from her spotless nails.

"The furies. Did you get a good look at them in his memories?"

"No. But you already knew that didn't you? If want to know who they are you're going to have to go to the library."

"Seriously?" I crossed my arms over my chest. "Like the library will help here. I'm not trying to write an essay."

"Hello," Shannon tapped her fingers to my forehead. "The library has genealogy records of fae in this area remember? It was covered our Freshman year." Shannon paused as her eyes widened. "Oh that's right you spent most of your year with Max. Of course you weren't paying attention."

Oh crap. Memories of Max in the library flooded my mind. My body ached as I thought of all the delicious things we did to each other between the shelves. A small smile slipped over my lips as the memory played on. I shook my head trying to clear the thoughts as I focused on Shannon.

"Library, right?"

"You might want to take him with you. It's possible he could help."

I glanced to Brandon drooling on the tile floor and shook my head. There was no way he would be of any use in the state he was in. But I certainly couldn't leave him in the hallway for some other Fae to finish him off. I dropped down and grabbed his arm. Pulling with all my might I hoisted him to his feet and slipped my arm around his waist.

"Come on then." Brandon mumbled incoherently in my ear as we moved slowly past Shannon.

"Don't ever leave me alone with her again," I managed to make out as we moved further down the hall.

"I shouldn't have left you alone. It was my fault."

"It's cool," Brandon hissed drunkenly. "Live and learn right?"

I nodded as I glanced over to him as we made our way out of the building and walked across campus. Every eye in the court was on us as I squeezed Brandon tighter to me. *How many of them wanted him and was simply holding back because he was with me?*

In the pit of my gut there came a bubbling. The warmth of his body so close to mine. Shannon's words spun around in my head like a carousel. *Was he something more than human? Would I find out anything from the records in the library?* There was only one way for me to know for certain. But what if Shannon was right? What if he was something more?

Glancing at him in the corner of my eye I wondered if he was more like me. *And if he was what would that mean?* I tried to push the thought from my head as I pulled open the large glass doors of the library. I already had Max and Luke, what the hell was I going to do with Brandon if he happened to be Fae too? Suddenly I really saw him.

His dark hair and soft almond shape eyes. His plump lips that hinted at a pout even if he smiled. It gave me the impression he wasn't sure how he felt. Still, from the moment I picked him up and brought him through the tunnel, there was a connection I didn't, no couldn't accept all because he was human. But now the possibility of him being something else blew me away.

No. Not until I know for certain. Pushing the desires and the thoughts out of my head I helped him to the large oak table in the middle of the library.

"Wait here," I ordered as he sloped down into the chair and his head dropped to the table.

"But," he started to protest as his eyes fluttered close. Glancing around I knew no one in here would dare make a move on him. But just to be certain I moved to his back and placed my hands on his shoulders. With my eyes narrowing on every face I saw I threw my shadow out of me and hovered over the slumbering Brandon.

"He's mine," I whispered so low that even I could barely hear it. But it was enough to cause the windows to rattle at my proclamation. The other's in the building all turned the heads down and stepped further from us. Slowly I pulled in my shadow and gasped as the weight of his soul pulled into me. I shivered feeling the new presences in me. It was almost intruding. Almost.

My eyes flashed to Brandon. The rise and fall of his chest as he slept calmed my nerves. Maybe Shannon was right about just getting some sleep. I leaned down and stared at him briefly before standing and moving towards the back of the library. I knew there, in the mess of dusty old books and volumes of forgotten lore I'd find my answers.

The hint of musk floated on the air as I moved through the tall shelves. My fingers ran over the dust covers as I searched for the genealogy books. I had no clue what I was looking for really, only that I had faith that I'd somehow find it waiting for me.

Chapter 6

"Fancy seeing you here."

I froze with my finger hovering on a dark cover. Pulling in a deep breath I glanced to find Max leaning against the shelf, his arms crossed over his broad chest and his eyes burning with lust.

"Surprise to see you here too," I said dropping my hand.

"I doubt that." He pushed off the shelf and moved closer to me. My heart raced as I watched him stalk me like a prey in the jungle.

"That was something," he said forcing his eyes off me to rub his fingers over the dusty book covers. For a moment I wondered if anyone came through here with a duster or just let these books sit and rot with time.

"What?" I took the bait before I could stop myself. I knew he was fishing for something and by the look in his eyes I could imagine what it was.

"You claimed that boy down there. Everyone in a ten-mile radius felt it."

"So? Maybe I didn't want anyone knocking him off before we got to the bottom of this?"

Max stalked my every move as he held me in place. There was something about his eyes that lured me into him. The way they pulled me into him. It wasn't just his physical body. Although it was nice to find him so well built. It was more than his smoldering glare as he stood but inches from me. Max was the first guy I was ever with. He could read me like a book and it was a story that evolved over time.

"What do you want Max?" I forced the words out as I turned to the bookshelf trying to push out all thoughts of the things we once did.

"Did you forget this is where we first met?" Max stepped closer to me, caging me against the bookshelf and his body. His body heat rolled off him and caressed me as I tried to steady my frantic heartbeat.

"Kira," my name rolled off his lips. Max's fingertips grazed over my hips as I swallowed trying to keep my head clear. "Tell me you don't want me, and I'll leave. Tell me right now."

Please, not right now. Don't do this right now.

"You wanted me earlier today, has so much changed? You must know what you do to me. How you tease me so."

"I don't have time for this Max." He knew as much as I did that I was lying. He pressed his body closer to mine and trapped me against the bookshelf.

"Tell Kira," his breath on my neck sent chills running over me. "Why did you really do it?"

I couldn't think as he dipped low to tickle this fingers under my skirt and hike up the denim fabric. With each inch he stole my head bobbed in the sea of uncertainty. My body ached for him as I closed my eyes allowing myself to succumb to his touch.

"What?" I managed to get out breathlessly. My fingers clung to the ledge of the bookshelf as if it were my life line. The last thing I wanted was to be swept under by Max's avalanche of lust. His hips pushed against mine and I could feel his bulging cock begging to be released.

With the sound of my heart pounding in my head I tried to find steady ground.

"You claimed a human," he said drifting his fingers between my inner thighs. He was so close to touching my pussy it was maddening.

"I don't think he is entirely human."

Did I seriously just say that out loud? Did I just let it slip? I turned my head as guilt filled me. Max's lips worked eagerly on my neck, soothing my fears as I'm sure he felt my body tense.

"Why do you think that?" he asked nibbling down to my shoulders. With one hand around my waist holding me in place and his other conquering the lower half of my body, there was no way I was thinking straight.

My head twitched back and forth as my lips drew into a tight line. I wasn't going to give away anymore secrets or accusations. Not until I knew the truth.

Max's fingers played at the hem of my panties as he pushed his hips once more into mine. "Keeping quiet, huh? Fine, you keep your secrets. But I'll get them out, eventually."

You can try.

I clung to the bookshelf and sucked in a quick breath as his fingertip pushed the elastic away. The shock of his skin on my pussy lips stunned me. Max always knew how to tease me, just as I knew how to play with him. I glanced over my shoulder trying to remember to breathe as he slipped his finger between the lips of my pussy.

"That's what I like to feel. Soft and delicate." He said tracing over the slit. My god, he knew how to tease. He applied just enough pressure to penetrate the outer lining, but never enough to slip into my body. It was the half way point that drove me insane and he knew it.

I wiggled my hips as my legs twitched. Every ounce of my being wanted him. I couldn't deny my body the pleasure of his touch. It wasn't like I wanted more, it was more the fact I needed it. He had pushed me so far over the edge that I couldn't think straight anymore.

The small sliver of the bookshelf that kept me clinging to my sanity failed. It was like the precipice failed and I tumbled down into the sea of lust tossed about with Max as my only vessel for navigating the torrential sea.

"Do you want me?" Max's words tickled my fancy like a life line. All I could do was nod my head as he pushed his fingers into my body. I gasped at the pressure of his quick penetration. He pumped his fingers in and out as my body responded in kind. I released the security of the bookshelf and dropped my arm. My fingers grazed over his thighs as I circled his legs to reach the zipper of his pants.

"Are you sure that is what you want right now?" Max asked. For a moment I wondered why he asked that. My eyes flickered about the room. Books and shelves rose high to the ceiling. The fluorescent lights flickered above our heads. We weren't in some closed off room of the school. We were in the library were any moment a student or faculty could walk around the corner to find us engaged in such taboo things.

Let them catch us. I don't care.

Oh how I thought those same words so long ago. But they were true today as they were so long ago. I didn't care what who walked over to us. I didn't care if the dean herself found us shagging like rabbits between the ancient books of the Fae. I wanted Max and by the stiffness of his cock between my fingers and his slacks, he wanted me too.

"Unleash me," he said. "Let me remind you of why you love me best."

I didn't hesitate. With the thin metal between my fingertips I pulled down his fly and quickly found my way into the slot of his pants. His cock was hard and ready for me. Carefully I maneuvered his dick up and through the small hole. His moan in my eat thrilled me.

"Squeeze me," he ordered. I curled my fingers around his shaft and tightening my grip around him. His entire body trembled under my touch as I stroked the length of him.

A moan slipped his lips as his fingers dug into my stomach. His cock throbbed in my hand as his fingers pushed and pumped to the rhythm I set.

"I want inside of you," he said.

Finally. I needed him to want me. My pussy pulsed with the thought of having his cock fill me up. Without warning his fingers slipped out of me, leaving behind a cold empty place between my legs. I could feel the moisture pooling in my panties as both his hands bolted to the hem of my shirt and hoisted the fabric to my hips.

Quickly he scrambled to my panties and shoved the thin fabric to the side as he swiped away my hand holding his cock. His body dropped a few inches as he pressed the head of his cock over the slit of my pussy searching for a way in.

I sucked in a sudden breath as the tip pushed into the hole between my legs. His thick veined cock lunged deeper in my body as my hands rose to the bookshelf for support.

God how I missed him. Every inch of his cock pushed the boundaries of my body and stretched me in ways I had nearly forgotten about. With each inch he stole I found myself moaning. His hands clung to my hips as his body bobbed and pushed until the length of his cock slipped into me effortlessly.

"Don't you say a word," he warned as the books on the shelf rattled and jerked with each thrust of his hips to mine.

Oh Max how I missed you. I've missed your girth filling me up and the way each pound of your hips into my pushes me closer to that edge.

I wanted to scream to moan with pleasure with each and every jerk. As his cock slipped out, I sighed in relief and in pain. He left a hole in me that couldn't be filled with anything but him. But just as quickly as he was gone, he returned. My body was thrust into the air lifting my feet off the ground as his cock anchored me to him.

"Don't you dare," he warned releasing his hands from my hips and curling one around my torso. His fingers pinched my hardened nipple as his other hand cupped over my mouth silencing my sounds.

The pressure of my pinched nipple rocked me to new levels of pleasure. He rolled his fingers about that sent chills pricking me everywhere. My eyes rolled back as his hand around my mouth stifled my noises. My pussy swelled and throbbed as the books rocked on the shelf.

A loud thump at the end of the row caused Max to pause for just a heartbeat. My eyes darted to the source of the sound. I spotted the thick volumes sprawled open, pages bent out of shape laying on the floor.

"Pity." Max was breathless as he jerked his body up and pulled my body down. His teeth grazed over my earlobe as he spoke, "I had hoped we'd get caught."

Brandon.

My eyes narrowed to spy between the thin open layer of space between the top of the shelf and the books that lined it. There sitting in his plastic blue chair hunched over on the table was Brandon. His hair flowed over his arm as he slumbered.

If he should catch me here with Max? My heart dropped into my stomach as I glanced over my shoulder at Max. His face was flushed as his body ravished mine. Each push sent chills through me. Every inch of his cock that filled me up taunted me. I clung to his pant legs as the thrill and excitement of Brandon catching us filled my mind. It was as if Max's darkest desires seeped into my head and made me want them too.

Damn it, the claiming always had ramifications. My heart cracked as my attention drifted back to Brandon. The human stirred in his seat and my eyes widened as Luke climbed the steps and paused.

Oh shit.

"Ohh now it's a party," Max huffed increasing his speed causing more books to fall from the shelf.

"Max," I pleaded as the tip of his cock rubbed against that tender bulb inside my body causing the lights to flicker around me. Dark spots began to cloud my vision as my grip on Max's pants tightened.

"Are you coming?" he teased as his hand around my mouth silenced me once more.

Every muscle in my body ached. Every fiber tingled as I lost all control of sight and sound. All I could see was the tunnel of light opening before me; the sweet hum of electricity filled my ears as my body trembled at Max's doing.

"That's my girl," he whispered as the light faded.

Before I could stop him, Max hoisted me off him and left me clinging to the bookcase for support.

"Go get yourself cleaned up before anyone sees you like this," he stated as I glanced over my shoulder to find him tucking his cock back into the slit of his pants.

Jerk.

But he was my jerk. I shook my head and spun around to spy through the shelves as I pulled down my skirt. My heart fluttered as Luke leaned over Brandon and pushed his finger into Brandon's shoulder.

He knows I'm here.

As I turned to look back at Max a wicked grin flashed over his lips. I could feel my juices seeping between my legs.

"Keep an eye on them will you?" I knew it was an impossible request, but I couldn't just stand there any longer. I had to get to the bathroom and clean myself up.

Max nodded as he crossed his arms over his chest, "Sure, I'll keep an eye on your human."

"Do not hurt him."

"You think so little of me." He pouted as he lifted one hand up and crossed his chest with his finger.

"I mean it Max."

"I wouldn't dream of hurting him."

"Yes you would," I said as I darted to down the aisle and made a sharp turn.

"There you are," Luke said as I careened into him.

Not now. I could feel my panties moistening with every second.

"Bathroom," I pointed to the ladies room behind Luke. He smiled and dipped his head as I raced around him and bolted into the cream colored room.

For a brief moment relief washed over me. I scurried to the open stall and slipped off my wet panties and quickly cleaned myself as I heard the squeak of the bathroom door opening.

"You know I don't mind your extra circular activities or anything with Max, but did you really have to keep it in the family?"

"Luke, this is the ladies room. And what are you talking about? Keep what in the family?"

"I know where I am, but it's not like I haven't this stuff before. And you and that Brandon." Luke flew his hand up in the air and shrugged. "I guess it really doesn't matter as long as I get you tonight. Alone."

"I haven't forgotten about tonight. But what do you know about Brandon?"

"I think that is something you should ask Max about." Questions burned within me as I stared up at Luke. His arms wrapped around my small frame as he brushed his hand down my cheek. His mouth opened to speak just as the bathroom door swung open. A blond haired sprite with her pale shimmering skin and emerald green eyes waltzed in.

"What the hell Luke! Get out."

"I guess that's my cue," Luke said smiling as he pressed his lips to my forehead.

"Wait, Luke. You need to tell me about Brandon." Luke pressed his lips together and pulled away as the young sprite slapped his arm and shoved him out the door.

"If I were you, I wouldn't leave Max alone with Brandon for too long. Sometimes bad things happen when brothers get together."

"Wait!"

"Get out Luke," the sprite grumbled until she pushed him out the door in one final heave.

Confusion. Shock. Everything was completely jumbled in my mind. Was Luke right? Was Brandon and Max related? That didn't make any sense. There was no way. Brandon was human and Max, well he was a son of Ares. I watched with wondered and awe at the bathroom door. If I was going to get answers I wasn't going to get them from Luke.

"Seriously Kira? How many times have you let a guy come in here? I should so report this."

Instinct took over as my shadow stretched past me and engulfed the poor sprite. "You aren't going to report anything."

Chapter 7

Flushed and spent, I pushed through the door and stumbled trying to wrap my head around Luke's words. I trembled at the thought of Brandon being Fae. I had hoped against hope that he was human, that all this would be done with the moment I tracked down the dark Fae. But as I put one wobbly foot before the other my eyes drifted between Max and Brandon.

The men stood shoulder to shoulder, full thick checks and long sturdy arms. Arms that could wrap a girl up and make all her fears melt away. Arms that could crush the most vile enemies in a single blow. I stood dumbstruck by the mouth of the aisle studying both with such scrutiny that my eyes must have been deceiving me.

As I stared, I noticed the bridge of their nose arched at the same angle, their cheeks rose high on their faces, and their expression as they caught me staring were nearly identical.

No way.

"You okay Kira?" Brandon asked as his eyes darted to Max before he took a step closer to me. I shook my head as my mouth dropped.

Did they know? Did either one of them have a freaking clue they were brothers? I clapped my hand over my mouth in shock, fearful of what might slip. Brandon, with his unsure footing and slow reflexes came to me.

No. No way. He moves too slowly. He can't be Fae. There is no way. But the longer I stared the more possible it became. There was no denying the resemblance he shared with Max. It was as plain as white bread. I swallowed hard as Luke's words haunted and frightened me.

"Ask Max," he said. "He'd tell me what I wanted to know."

Carefully I stepped closer to Max my eyes flickering between the two. Max stood like a mountain. His shoulders drew back as his eyebrow rose. The smug grin plastered on his face caused me to pause.

He really thought he was the god's gift to women.

"Kira, you're looking a bit peaked. Maybe you should sit down and rest a few moments," Max said, his eyes narrowing in on me. Brandon wrapped his arm around my waist and led me to the closest chair.

I plopped down in the seat as Brandon held it steady for me. Shifting my weight I wondered how to break the news.

No. That wasn't how to do it. I need to be certain. I wasn't about to just blurt out, hey you two are brothers did you know? It had to be done with finesse.

I sucked in a deep breath to steady my nerves as Brandon walked around me and sat in the seat adjacent to mine. He reached across the table to take my hands. Shocked, I hadn't realized they were trembling.

"You know Kira, you really should try to get more exercise," Max huffed chuckling to himself as Brandon glanced over his shoulder to him. Brandon shook his head as he glared at Max.

"What?" Max huffed throwing his arms out like he was ready for a fight.

"Max," his name felt like a dry piece of toast in my throat. His eyes found me and he stopped to really look at me. Once I had his undivided attention, I swallowed the lump of fear filling my throat.

"How did you know you were what you are?" I asked. The words fumbled from my lips as I spoke them. Still, it didn't seem real or possible. Max's answer though would tell me if I was crazy or if Luke was lying.

"What are you talking about?"

"How did you know you were Fae? Were you born this way? Did you wake up one day and realize you had gifts? Was it a puberty thing? What?" I slammed my hand on the table, rage filling me up that I could taste death on my tongue. I had to reel in my emotions before I laid waste the population within the library.

"Seriously? You're bringing that up? I didn't tell you when you first asked and I am certainly not going to tell you now with a human in the room."

"Max," I dropped my shoulders and my eyes. I didn't want to force the answer out of him although we both knew I could. "Please. Just tell me. Were you attacked?"

Max paused and rubbed his chin as I saw the wheels in his head spinning. A light of recognition flickered in his eyes and I knew the answer before he said a word.

"Pops has a sick sense of humor. He really likes to play with people you know? I had banshees come for me when I was 13. Do you have any idea what it's like to hear those gals screaming at you?"

I dropped further into my seat and exhaled slowly as I slipped my hand out of Brandon's grasp.

"You okay?" Brandon asked leaning back in his chair as I pressed my lips into a tight line.

"The dark fae are here to trigger your gifts. To prove you are a son of Ares," I blurted.

"What?" Brandon and Max said in unison. I looked up, defeated as I glanced at Max first, then Brandon.

"Ares controls Furies right?" My eyes flickered to Max for the answer. Max's head bobbed as Brandon glanced over his shoulder.

"Brandon, you have fae blood running through your veins. Ares is your father. He shacked up with your mom. That is why they are after you."

"That's not possible," Brandon shook his head as Max's mouth dropped.

"My dad left my mom before I was born."

"That's his M.O." Max said in a hushed tone that even I could barely hear.

"Look, I don't know what they will do to you, or even if they have permission to kill you."

"Wait, what? Kill me are you freaking serious?" Brandon shot up from his chair and bounced around as he ran his fingers through his hair. He paced the open floor shaking his head as he mumbled.

"With the Fae it is black and white. Either they trigger a response out of you and you defend yourself, or you die."

"I can't do this," Brandon twitched and turned. Terror molded onto his face as he stalked from one row of tables to the next and back again.

"You have to." Max for once was the voice of reason. My eyes shot to him as he grabbed Brandon by the shoulders forcing him to stop his pacing.

"Look, I don't know if we are brothers or not, honestly I think it would be kind of cool. But you need to chill out for a moment. I have been through this before. It may seem impossible, but trust yourself and you will make it through. Got me?"

Wow. Max held Brandon's gaze, and I saw the fire and brimstone, the eternal inferno forging up through the pits of hell. Max was born to take charge, born to lead. No wonder I claimed him so long ago. I hadn't seen the fire in him in nearly three years. Yet here it was burning brighter than ever.

"Brandon, listen to me," I rose from my seat and joined the boys in the middle of the library. I placed my hands on top of Max's and shot him a quick reassuring glance before turning my attention to Brandon. "Breathe for me."

He pulled in a deep breath and released it slowly as I held his gaze. I nodded as I mimicked his breathing pattern.

"Every son of Ares goes through this. I won't lie, some have died because the gene wasn't strong enough to be triggered."

"Oh god," Brandon pulled in a quick terrified gulp of air.

"But I know where they go afterward. I bring them to their final resting place."

"And where is that?" Brandon asked, his voice wavering.

"She's a Valkyrie dude, where do you think she'll take you?" Max said as my eyes darted to him.

"Valhalla," Brandon answered. Max clamped down on Brandon's shoulders, a scene I hadn't seen since the Vikings cheered on their noble warriors.

Staring at Brandon I could tell Max's words and his sure tone settled Brandon's uneasiness. With each passing moment a soothing calm drifted over Brandon's features.

"Is it really as pretty as they say it is?" Brandon asked turning his attention to me. I couldn't help but shrug. Perhaps I had seen it one too many times. Or maybe it just didn't have the same effect on me as it did others. I didn't know. But I forced a smile and shook my head. Who was I to crush a man's dreams?

"Besides," Max laughed as I dropped my hands from Brandon's shoulders. "It's not like you have to face them now. The furies aren't even here, now are they?"

The crash of glass and the moan of wood scrapping across the floor shattered the silence of the library. My wings emerged before I could stop them and covered Max and Brandon under their protective umbrella.

Shards of glass, books, tables, all the stuff lining the side of the library flew through the air like a comet struck the side of the library. I couldn't help but whimper as the noise pierced my ears.

"You just had to say it didn't you?" I asked whipping my head to Max. He shrugged as the squeal of the furies filled the two story building.

"Bring us the human."

Chapter 8

There was a wildness in Brandon's eyes, a fear that had no name. He quaked next to me as I tried to shake the fear from him.

"Brandon, you have to face them."

He shook his head and dropped his eyes, "I can't."

"Yes, you can. I did it with the banshees you can do it with the furies," Max said patting Brandon on the shoulder as my eyes flickered to the open windows.

Dark billowed clouds swirled around in the sky. Lightening crackled between the clouds as students screamed, ducking for cover. I stood with my wings out as flames danced between the clouds and the ground. Pillars of smoke and flames swirled about as fear seeped into me.

So this is what it feels like.

I shook my head and closed my eyes. Furies could make heaven hell in their victim's minds. And that was precisely what they were doing now. The more I concentrated the more I found the weak link in their illusion. No one, not even a Fury could possess the mind of a Valkyrie. Their cheap parlor tricks had nothing on me.

I pushed against the darkest with my shadow as Max gasped. I couldn't look at him, I couldn't let anything break my concentration or the furies would have their way with our minds once again.

"Whatever you're doing, keep doing it," Max said. In the corner of my eye I spied him rising to his feet and pulling Brandon up with him.

"Kira is a solider of the light," Max explained. "As long as she keeps their darkness at bay, you can defeat these creatures of hell." Brandon winced as Max slapped his hand down on Brandon's shoulder.

"Are you with me?" Max asked.

Hold on. You can do this. But with each passing moment I could feel myself slipping. Granted I knew what I was capable of, but it was just me against three. If Brandon didn't make up his mind soon, I would fail.

"Kira, give us as much time as you can. Brandon here is about to get a crash course on Fae magic."

"Hurry up guys, I got three of them against me right now."

"Come on," Max said as he grabbed Brandon by the collar and lead him over the broken glass and outside.

My heart raced and splintered as I watched them walk outside without me. I could only hope that I had enough strength to protect their minds against the furies. The last thing I wanted was to lose either one of them to the depths of hell. Guilt flickered through my mind. Self-doubt too.

No. You. Don't.

If there was one thing I knew it was doubt. The furies weren't playing nicely as they continued to attack me by any means necessary. But casting doubt was my gift not theirs.

I sucked in a deep breath and held it in my lungs waiting for the burning sensation to prick my lungs. I could taste the death on my tongue as my shadow slipped out of me and drifted towards the shattered windows. If they wanted to know what death was like for real, they were about to get a taste of it.

"Kira NO!"

The sound of my name startled me. It wasn't Max who called for me, or Brandon, but a whimsically light and airy voice that belong to Luke. Luke, of course the son of Apollo could never be trapped in the darkness. His own light would shine through and cast the shadows to the ends of the earth. But I wasn't worried about Luke. He could handle himself against the agents of hell. No. It was Brandon and Max, brothers who play so close to the edge that they could fall into temptation so easily. It was them I cast my shadow to. It was them I wanted to protect.

"Kira stop! Please." Luke pleaded as I felt his fingers curl around my shoulders. The lingering sourness of death caked my tongue as I swallowed.

"NO!"

My eyes flickered to the shadows emerging like smoke through the open windows. Luke held me close as all the shouting and cries faded into the back of my mind. A brilliant flash of light flooded my sight forcing me to raise my hand to my face to protect my vision.

"Why did you stop me? I could have saved him," I said to Luke as I stared up into his beautiful face. His eyes glowed like the moonlight on a dark night as his fingers stroked my hair and drifted down my face.

"Brandon has to do this alone or his powers won't come, you know this."

"But there are three of them," I huffed as a searing white hot poker stabbed my shoulder. I pulled my eyes off Luke to find a dark arrow dissolving in my shoulder.

"MAX!" Luke's voice carried over the smoke and ruins with such an urgency that is caused my blood to run cold.

"Kira's been hit."

The thunderous No boomed over the screams and panic. My throat dried as I tried to focus on stretching my shadow out further still. Yet with each push, I found myself wincing. Pain and regret flowed over me as the tunnel of light swirled above my head before opening. I fell back into Luke's arms as Brandon and Max raced to my side.

"How did this happen?" Max asked tracing his fingers over my body until he paused at the festering wound at my shoulder.

"She was casting her shadow out to push back the furies influence to help you," Luke said, his eyes flickering to Brandon before falling back on me. "The arrow came out of nowhere and struck her."

"It dissolved didn't it?" Max said brushing his fingers over my sweaty forehead. Luke's head bobbed as Brandon dropped his head.

"You guys," I gasped as my eyes remained locked on the swirling light above my head. "I'll be fine."

"Please don't leave," Brandon whispered.

"This is your fault human," Max said shoving Brandon away from me. "If you would have just done what I told you, this wouldn't have happened."

"Please guys don't fight," I mumbled as I tried to lift my hand up to Max. But the weight was far too much, and it dropped like stones at my side.

"Kira please don't go," Luke said as Max tried to draw out the poison in my shoulder.

"It's too late for me." My body grew heavy as my shadow drifted out of me effortlessly towards the tunnel of light.

"Kira, please," Max's voice broke as I drifted away from him and hovered in the ether. I stared down at my beloveds. The strong warrior with the devil may care attitude, but fierce and undying loyalty. The caring, tender selfless poet who carried me through my darkest nights. And then the human, the helpless, fragile human whom I never would have thought to care for.

Yet, here I am, my heart breaking for them all as the furies unleashed their powers. I wish I could do more. But it was too late, the halls of Valhalla rose through the light as my sisters called me home.

"She isn't going to die in vain," Brandon hissed turning his back to Max. Red angry light broke through the darkness and the veil as I watched Brandon unleash his inner Fae. My mouth dropped as my heart swelled with pride to see him come into his own. I wish I could be there to congratulate him, but it wasn't meant to be. His victory was his own.

"Well done sister." A soothing voice called out to me as I rose ever higher through the marble pillars towards the great hall. Brandon, Max, Luke, Tartarus High, all of it soon was washed out by the light. A piece of me crumbled to dust.

Chapter 9

"Welcome, Kira Adams." The voice was loud but by no means intrusive. My eyes scanned the great hall as only Valkyrie stood proudly around me. At the front of the mighty room two women stood side by side. Their wings were opened like arms to welcome me to them.

Every fiber in my being wanted to go to them, want to rush to the women and wrap my arms around their necks and never leave. Love and companionship trickled through my body as my heart swelled. I was home. For the first time in forever I felt as if I belong among these magnificent women. All who kept their eyes on me as I moved down the rows.

"Do you know where you are?" the woman to the right asked. The closer I got the better my eyes could see through her blinding light. Her hair was white as snow, her lips ruby red and her eyes blue as ice. I stepped closer to find her skin was like crystal, transparent and hard yet ever so welcoming.

"Valhalla," I answered as the crowd cheered.

"I am Astrid," the woman on the right said as she lowered her head and bowed to greet me. Odd that she would dip to me. By the looks of her and the way others stared at her with such fondness I had thought she was the queen of the Valkyries.

"Hi," I lifted my hand to give a quick wave as I looked to the woman at her right. The woman looked awfully familiar. Her hair wasn't as white as Astrid's, in fact half was black. Her skin was golden like bronze and her eyes locked on me as if they drew me closer to her like a magnet.

"This is Olivia," Astrid said smiling. "Brandon's mother."

"But you're a Valkyrie," I said stunned. My eyes widened as recognition struck me. She was the soul I had to claim. The one who begged me to take care of Brandon. It was her no doubt, but it wasn't. She looked so different and I couldn't place her at all.

"How is this possible? I brought you to your resting place. You… You were human."

"Half human yes," Olivia said tugging at the black strands of hair. Clearly they were a marking of what she once was and what she gave up.

"How is that possible? There are no half breed Valkyries."

"You're right Kira, there is not. But that doesn't mean that we as women can't love?"

"We can't it is not in our nature to feel such things. We are harsh, but fair. How would our reputations be if we picked sides on the battle field? How would it be if we could control where souls went once they were dead?"

"Oh Kira," Astrid sighed as she exchanged a meaningful glance to Olivia. "Sometimes I forget how young you really are."

"What does that supposed to mean?" I could feel my blood boiling as I spoke with Astrid. Her condescending tone irritated me as she stepped down and placed her hand on my shoulder.

"We know you haven't picked a side. Or should I say, picked one too many."

"What are you talking about? I haven't picked any sides. I am a Valkyrie." Fear, doubt, confusion filled me as Astrid moved swiftly around me. Her smile grew as she studied every inch of me as she passed.

"You have chosen three to be yours have you not? Three splinters of souls that remain in your possession." Astrid waved her hand in the air as three bulbs of light emerged out of my chest. As each ball popped out of me I could feel their emptiness.

I whipped my hands up trying to claim them once more before Astrid could burst the colorful bubbles. But it was no use. They were just out of reach and I was vulnerable to Astrid's whim. If she wanted to, she could vanquish the bubbles floating above me.

"This one," Astrid sighed as she called the yellow ball of light down to me. "This is your sun. Yes. I can see that now. He fills you with peace and tranquility."

I glanced up to find Luke's smiling face staring at me through the soft yellow light. His eyes stunning even in this form drew me in. How I wished he was here now, holding me and whispering such things to easy my nerves.

"You love him yes?" Astrid asked. I pressed my lips into a tight line as a single tear swelled in the corner of my eye. If I admitted the truth, she would pop it. If I didn't, she would dispose of it, anyway. No matter which way I answered I would lose.

Keeping my mouth shut I crossed my arms and glared at her. If she was about to set me free of those I claimed, I would bring down the walls. The ground rumbled under my feet as a smile played at the corner of her lips.

"And what of this one? Fierce and feisty. He is unpredictable and cunning. No wonder why you picked him." The red ball looped and flipped as Astrid called it down. My Max. His eyes were so sure, so cocky that there was no wrong decision with him. No reason for doubt. I pulled in a deep breath trying not to give away my emotions.

"Then there is this one," Astrid said calling down the blue bulb that flickered from blue to white and back again. "He is the voice of reason for you I see."

"Get to the point. If you are going to pop them, then do it. If not put them back," I demanded as I spread open my wings. Growls and hisses encompassed me but I didn't care. I would fight every last sister I had to keep my treasures.

"Interesting," Astrid said turning her attention of Olivia. "You don't realize what these are do you?"

I held my stance waiting for the shoe to drop. Clearly this was some sort of test and I was failing. My eyes darted to the others circling around me refusing to let them take an inch of ground.

"I couldn't pop these if I wanted," Astrid said, her smile widening. "This proves that you are in love."

"What? I don't love."

"Really? Astrid's eyebrows rose in suspicion. "You got awfully defensive about them when you thought they could be easily disposed of. Even now you are waiting for some drastic thing to occur so you can avenge their loss aren't you?"

I stepped back dumbfounded. The woman could read my mind.

"Kira, that is what happens when you live among the flesh," Olivia said stepping closer to me. Her arms stretched out, and she wrapped them around me as she continued, "Your heart has awakened and so has your true Valkyrie powers."

Astrid smiled as the balls of light floated and swirled around me. "Love is the greatest power we possess. Will you accept this power? Or deny it?"

I stared at the balls of light and studied each one. The red glow of Max filled me with such strength that I realized I wouldn't be the girl I am today without him. He was my shield and my rock. I reached out my hand and summoned the ball to me. As I closed my eyes and thought of Max, I opened my heart.

The void that once pricked me was warm and inviting. I exhaled as the love mended me in ways I couldn't explain. *Astrid was right, I did love Max and would die defending him.*

I turned my sights to the golden bronze ball and called it to me. Closing my eyes I allowed the ball to pierce the darkness of my soul and fill me with hope and faith. Luke was my own personal sun. He was warm and kindness and everything that held me together when things got bad. There was no way I could live without such a light in my life.

"My son is still new to all this," Olivia said as I called the bluish ball to me. I glanced at her and nodded once as I stared at the light. "Please don't tell me about me. Not yet anyway."

"He'll find out eventually," I said holding the light to my chest.

"I know. But it doesn't have to be any time soon does it? There is just so much he needs to learn first."

"I'll do my best to keep the secret," I said as a faint hint of a smile played at the corner of her lips.

"Treat him good," Olivia said as I pulled Brandon's light into me.

With my heart filled and my love restored I was lighter than air. Even the golden light of the halls of Valhalla couldn't penetrate me. I was finally whole as I wept with joy.

"You have a choice Kira," Astrid said as she touched my cheek with the back of her hand. "You can go back and be their lover. Or you may go back as a human and experience love for yourself."

"I don't understand," I said turning to Olivia. Olivia pulled the stark black strands of her hair as she smiled.

"Your love for these men cannot get in the way of your duty to your nature. You are a Valkyrie and with that comes responsibility. You cannot skirt that duty. But you can give it up right now," Astrid said as she turned to the fair girl in the corner.

The young Valkyrie rushed to Astrid's side holding a pair of sheers in her hand. The silver shimmered in the light as the girl passed them to Astrid.

"I can clip your wings," Astrid said.

"But then you will be like me," Olivia stated. "Only half Valkyrie. Part human which is frail and weak but that can love tremendously."

"It's your call," Astrid said as she held up the pair of scissors ready to snip away my immortality.

I paused looking at the silver gleam in Astrid's hand as I pressed my lips into a tight line. I could feel every ounce of love from Max, Luke, and Brandon and wished they could be here right now to help me make this decision.

But they weren't. This was something I would have to do on my own.

I sucked in a deep breath and turned to Astrid, "I'm sorry, but I'm not ready to give my wings up. Not yet."

Astrid's head bobbed, "I figured as much."

"So what happens now?" I asked looking around the room. The light burned brighter and washed out Astrid and Olivia as well as the other Valkyries. My sisters.

In a flash of lightening and a crack of thunder I found myself huddled in a ball under the bleachers. Darkness had come, and the moon was lingering on the horizon practically kissing it.

"There you are." The familiar voice soothed my fear as I rose to my feet.

"Luke?"

"Who did you think I was?" he chuckled as he held a pile of clothes in his arms. I stared at him confused as he handed me the garments.

"Thought you might need these," he said blushing. I glanced down only to find my bare skin exposed to the elements. "Of course if I was Max, I might take advantage of this situation."

"Good thing you're not, huh?" I said snatching the clothes and throwing them on. It was good to see some things never changed.

"What happened after…" I didn't have to finish, Luke knew what I was talking about. He sucked in a deep breath and stuffed his hands into his pockets.

"Max and Brandon got into it for a bit. Then they took their angry out on those Furies. Of course Brandon didn't know you were coming back. He's new to all this. But, after Max explained, Brandon cooled off. He's in the dorms waiting for you. As for the furies, I doubt they will be attacking again anytime soon."

"Let's hope not."

"Did you find out what you needed to know while you were gone?" Luke asked winking. I shook my head as my favorite crooked smile played at the corner of his lips.

"Maybe," I said nudging my shoulder into his.

He wrapped his arms around me and held me close, pressing his lips to my forehead.

"You know I love you right?" he asked squeezing me. My heart swelled as I returned the hug and held him tighter.

"I know and I-"

"I know."

Epilogue

"Well done ladies," Ares clapped his hands as two of the Furies stood before him as he paced the marble balcony. His eyes burned with delight with each passing moment.

"We lost a sister," Set said crossing her arms defiantly.

"I promised you all great things if you succeeded. Great things," Ares said rubbing his hands together as the two remaining sisters glanced at one another.

"My dearest Delphine is in the underworld making preparations. She knew her part. Now my dear furies, there is much more to be done."

"Are you telling me she knew what you were up to and still went along with it?" Set's eyes flickered to Arae before shifting back to Ares.

"Of course she knew what my plans are. Do you really think me so unprepared? I couldn't very well send her on this mission without some kind of purpose. And right now, she is fulfilling her promise to me. Everything is set and the stakes are raised. My boys will soon be unstoppable."

"But-" Set began as she raised her arm out only to have Ares vanish in puff a smoke. The hint of sulfur lingered behind as Set turned to Arae.

"I don't know about you, but I'm starting to not trust him," Set said glaring off the balcony as dark clouds swayed and twisted in the ashen sky.

"Something wicked is coming this way," Arae said stepping back from the edge of the balcony. The sky danced and flickered with lightening as the clouds blew in from the south. The electricity in the air caused the hair on the back of the furies necks to rise. The sisters shivered and caught each other's eye.

"Do you feel it?" Arae asked rubbing her hands against her arms as the temperature dropped around them.

"Yeah, I feel it," Set said with her eyes locked on the shimmering veil. "And something tells me, those boys are going to be in the eye of the storm."

"Should we warn them?" Arae asked as the frigid air chilled her.

"We need to wait for Ares to make his move first. Right now, we have bigger issues. Like getting Delphine out of Hades."

THE END